1: *Heavenly Cauliflowers*

DAD WAS LATE.

Ned was nervous, waiting for his father's little Citroen to surge into Osborne Street. Their bags had been waiting in the hall since Ned got home from school.

Part of Ned was wild to spend a weekend with his dad. But most of him was terrified and kept cooking up excuses to stay behind. Suddenly, with a feeling like going down too fast in a lift, Ned remembered the real reason he couldn't go. "What if I have that dream?" he muttered.

"Then tell Dad, you nit," said Rose. "He hasn't turned into a werewolf just because he doesn't live with us."

Rose sounded cooler than a cucumber, but she was brushing her hair for the tenth time so Ned knew she was nervous too.

"What's so bad about stupid old heavenly cauliflowers anyway?" his big sister went on. "They won't eat you."

Ned couldn't explain that the dream which woke him yelling most nights was not a nightmare. It was magical, a message meant only for him. The sun shone. Birds sang in the apple trees. Bees buzzed in the bean-flowers. And the vegetables in Grandad's heavenly allotment were brighter and juicier than the old man had ever grown in his earthly one.

But the best thing was Grandad

ANTELOPE

Ugly Mug

by

ANNIE DALTON

Illustrated by Kate Aldous

HAMISH HAMILTON

LONDON

This book is for my son Reuben,
joint-rescuer of 'the boid',
and for Alex Ferguson, with love.

HAMISH HAMILTON LTD

Published by the Penguin Group
27 Wrights Lane, London w8 5tz, England
Penguin Books USA Inc., 375 Hudson Street, New York, New York 10014, USA
Penguin Books Australia Ltd, Ringwood, Victoria, Australia
Penguin Books Canada Ltd, 10 Alcorn Avenue, Toronto, Ontario, Canada m4v 3b2
Penguin Books (NZ) Ltd, 182–190 Wairau Road, Auckland 10, New Zealand

Penguin Books Ltd, Registered Offices: Harmondsworth, Middlesex, England

First published in Great Britain 1994 by Hamish Hamilton Ltd

Text copyright © 1994 by Annie Dalton
Illustrations copyright © 1994 by Kate Aldous

1 3 5 7 9 10 8 6 4 2

The moral rights of the author and artist have been asserted.

British Library Cataloguing in Publication Data
CIP data for this book is available from the British Library

ISBN 0-241-13377-7

Set in 15pt Baskerville by Rowland Phototypesetting Ltd
Bury St Edmunds, Suffolk
Printed and bound in Great Britain by
Butler & Tanner Ltd, Frome and London

Garfield himself, pottering between rows of spuds and baby carrots. His hair still stuck up in soft snowy spikes like a mischievous baby's. His eyes still sparkled. Only now he was well again, with the same healthy glow as his cauliflowers.

Ned never remembered what they said to each other. The important part, the part he'd never told anyone, came next, when Grandad gave a whistle so sweetly piercing that right in the middle of his dream Ned shivered. And with a whir of wings a small bird swooped from the trees to perch on Grandad's shoulder.

Then his grandfather said, "Hold out your hand, Ned." He said it seriously, as though he specially wanted Ned to remember it when he woke. "I've got something for you."

The dream was ending. Soon Ned would be alone again. Yet shakily he held out his hand. And the bird flew straight to Ned, settling on his palm with claws as scratchily-real as Mum's pan scourers. It eyed Ned with its head on one side, as if wondering what to make of him.

"Don't forget," Grandad always said then, fading as Ned stared at the bird, afraid to breathe. "Don't forget . . . "

Then it was over and Ned was

thrashing around yelling, "Don't go!"

There were so many things he never remembered to ask. Like *what* mustn't Ned forget?

Until Grandad died he and Ned had been best friends. Grandad understood Ned better than anyone else in the world. If he was alive he'd have stopped Mum and Dad splitting up, Ned thought. He'd have made them see what a mistake it was.

Ned remembered a new worry: "Does Dad know I'm vegetarian now?"

"He should do," said Rose. "You tell us often enough."

She faked a yawn and started shining her shoes. Bossy Rose was only eighteen months older than Ned, but since their parents had separated, she bossed Ned worse than ever. No one else noticed. Rose was careful to act specially helpful and grown-up around Mum, making Ned look lazy and babyish. And with Dad she danced about chattering and laughing like a happy little girl in a film, while Ned got more and more tongue-tied and sulky. Somehow, whichever parent she was with, Rose always got to be the good, special child. That meant Ned had to be the troublesome one. There was no one else left for him to be.

"Dad didn't remember about you hating mushrooms," Ned pointed out. "He seems to be forgetting about us."

Ned was afraid he was forgetting about Dad too. He'd lie in bed trying to remember the sound of his father's voice.

"He phones you every day," Mum pointed out. She glanced out of the window. Still no car.

"Dad won't know what to do with us, Mum." Ned was desperate. "Half the time he never listens to us."

Once, to test him, Ned repeated the same news in exactly the same words he used the last time Dad phoned, and Dad didn't notice.

"It's not easy for him either, you know, Ned," said Mum.

Ned kicked a chair-leg. That was another thing that muddled him up inside, the way Mum talked so kindly

about Dad these days. Did she think Ned didn't remember the fights and the shouting? Now, to hear Mum, you'd think she and Dad were best friends!

Except that they lived on opposite sides of town.

"We've got to sleep on air-beds," said Ned despairingly. "I'll wake up when I turn over. I'll be too tired to go to school on Monday."

"He's not a millionaire," said Mum, refusing to play this game. "He can't manage everything."

"He bought a flipping piano." Sometimes Ned wondered if he'd been kidnapped by cunning strangers who only *looked* like his real family. These days no one could give him a straight answer. Why wouldn't Mum admit their father just didn't CARE about

8

his children the way he used to?

"How would he write songs without a piano, stupid," said Rose, polishing furiously. "Do you want him to starve?"

Ned glared. "Those shoes will catch fire."

"Just because I'm not a scruffy toad."

"I'd rather be scruffy than blind people with my toe-caps."

9

Mum ignored them. "Come on, Ned," she said. "Remember the fun you two had? You went round being gangsters for an entire week once. You drove me crazy."

She laughed. Ned felt a surge of hope. But all he saw in her eyes was the tired expression she always wore these days.

Mum didn't want to stay married to Dad. She'd told them one terrible bedtime months ago. Dad didn't want to stay married to her, either. She'd explained it very calmly. As if a family was some bit of old knitting people could unpick without hurting anyone.

Then, Ned and Rose had had to go and brush their teeth as usual. That didn't seem right to Ned. There should have been a smoking hole in the middle of Osborne Street. There should have been screams, ambulances, flashing lights. Not this careful niceness that left Ned feeling crazy inside.

The trouble was that Mum wanted Ned to treat Dad the same as before. Even though they lived in different streets and had to arrange to meet like strangers. Even though Ned woke every morning to a new scared feeling in his stomach.

But Ned would never be the same again. And it just wasn't fair of Mum to try to make him.

A Citroen purred round the corner like an oversized sewing machine, braking with a shriek that had neighbours rushing to their windows, checking for squashed cats.

"At last," said Mum.

Rose dashed to the door. "It's my

daddy!" she yelled, in her excited little-girl voice.

She sounds like flipping Heidi, Ned thought bitterly.

Dad was in the hall, smiling his old lopsided smile. "Ready, you two?" he said. "Say goodbye to your mum, Ned."

But Ned glowered, refusing to look back. Mum might be able to make him go, he thought. But she couldn't make him *like* it, could she?

2: Murder Burgers

"YOU CAN POP round when you like, Ned," said Dad, as he parked the car. "Now I've got a place of my own."

"I might have too much homework," said Ned in a bored voice. It was the first thing he'd said since they left Osborne Street.

"Bring it," Dad suggested. "You used to like me helping with your maths."

"I do it by myself now," said Ned. "Thanks."

"Oh, I see," said his father.

Rose patted his hand. "I can't do

14

maths for toffee. You can still help me." When she wasn't busy being Heidi, Rose sometimes fussed over Dad, as if divorce was a terrible illness Dad might die of if she wasn't careful.

"Is this where you live?" demanded Ned. He stared disbelievingly at the peeling brown paint and the ugly porthole over the porch.

"I love it," said Rose at once. "It's got – character."

Ned rolled his eyes.

Dad grinned. "Wait till you meet Gretta," he said. "Now she *has* got character. Give me a hand with the groceries, you two. I stopped off at Sainsburys to make sure I had all your favourite nosheroni."

Ned had forgotten the way Dad made up silly food words. Nosheroni. Nosheretti. Nosheroodle.

"It smells funny," complained Ned, lugging his bags into the brown-painted hall.

"Not funny," corrected Dad. "Different. It's suppertime so you can smell cooking. Gretta's smells best of all. Sometimes I can hardly drag myself past her door. If you're in luck she'll let you try her delicious *piroshki*."

That was twice Dad had mentioned Gretta. Ned's father had only been here a fortnight and already he'd got a foreign girlfriend. No wonder he'd forgotten them. Ned blinked hard, squinting at his groceries and hoping there'd be something he could eat.

Recently Ned had decided to be vegetarian. Unfortunately he didn't actually like vegetables. It wasn't Ned's fault. He was trying to *learn* to like them.

16

They were climbing brown stairs, past brown wallpaper. Even the cracked ceiling was brown. Ned cricked his neck trying to see how much further there was to go. His arms were nearly out of their sockets.

"One more flight," panted Dad. "It was fun getting the piano up here, I can tell you."

If Dad's flat was brown inside as well, Ned was going to die.

Dad unlocked the door. "Ta-ra!" he said, out of breath.

Ned's mouth fell open. He'd been wrong about the brown. Dad's sitting room was whiter than a hospital. And there was no furniture in it!

Rose dug Ned fiercely in the ribs. "It's so *spacious*, Daddy," she said quickly.

"You're my first guests," beamed Dad.

Oh yeah, thought Ned, remembering the girlfriend. Aloud he demanded grouchily, "Where do you sit? What do you eat off?"

"We'll have to picnic until I get a table," said Dad. "Think you can cope?"

"We won't mind," said Rose airily. "We've got miles too much clutter at Osborne Street anyway."

Dad grinned. "That's true."

"No it isn't!" Ned was furious. Dad thought his old home was cluttered did he? Cluttered with *children* maybe. "Mum's house is just right," he growled. Dad's flat looked like a flipping aircraft hangar.

Dad wasn't a real father, that's what was wrong with him. Real fathers lived in the same house and listened when their children told them things. Real

fathers had proper cars instead of
yellow sewing machines full of dents.
They had carpet too, not horrible rush
matting everywhere.

In Dad's bleak white room there
were only books on metal shelves, a
piano, a few fat cushions, a thin
hungry lamp like a preying mantis,
and a droopy plant the size of a small
tree.

"What's that old tree for?" growled
Ned.

"It's a plant, stupid," corrected Rose.

"Ned's right," said Dad. "It's a weeping fig. It was too big for the last people to move."

"It's got a lot of dead leaves," said Rose. "Do you water it?"

"Of course," said Dad. "Well – I *meant* to."

"It's stupid, having a tree," said Ned sourly.

Dad disappeared through a door. "Oh, I don't know," he called. "I needn't buy a Christmas tree. I can hang decorations on this one instead. Bring everything through, troops."

"Troops," was Mum's word. It felt funny hearing Dad say it.

The kitchen was a dark cupboard, wallpapered with hideous giant peppers and sweet-corn. There were stains in the sink.

Ned pulled a face. "Man-eating vegetables," he hissed. Rose giggled. Ned was relieved. Even Rose didn't like the wallpaper.

"This was trendy in the Nineteen Fifties," said Dad. "Another few years and it'll be antique." He fished down a frying pan.

Ned groaned as he realised what else was missing from Dad's flat. "You haven't even got a telly." How would he survive a weekend?

"It's in my bedroom," explained Dad. "I'll bring it through if there's something you want to watch. It's only a little black and white portable, but as you know Ned, all the best films are already in black and white."

Unwillingly Ned smiled, remembering Sunday afternoons in

Osborne Street. Musicals, mysteries,
gangster films. Dad loved them all.
He'd go around saying, "See you
around, Schweetheart," to Mum, like
Humphrey Bogart. Or he'd talk out of
the corner of his mouth like Jimmy
Cagney. "You dirty rat," he'd say.

Ned loved the gangster films too. He
loved the way the characters talked,
saying "goil" instead of girl. The
gangsters had sweet names like
Babyface and Billy de Angelo, or
dangerous-sounding ones like The
Godfather.

Once Ned was bullied by a boy who
called him "Ugly Mug". When Ned
complained, Dad said immediately,
"Ugly Mug, what a great name for a
gangster!" and Ned was never scared
of the boy again.

Ned's smile vanished. He'd seen

what Dad was doing. "What are you cooking?" he croaked.

"Chips and burgers, of course." Dad put on his chef voice. "Not only am I preparing for you crinkle-cut chips; not only am I frying for you the best burgers Sainsburys have to offer, I am also making my own spicy sauce to accompany them. I can faithfully promise monsieur a meal to remember."

He went on cheerfully stripping bloody paper from the gristly slabs in front of him.

The blood left Ned's face. "You're cooking MEAT," he whispered. "You *don't* listen, Dad, do you? You don't remember the first thing about us. You just don't care any more."

"Ned doesn't eat meat now, Daddy," said Rose anxiously. "Never mind. Ned can eat chips, can't you Ned?'' Rose was wearing the expression she got when Ned threw up in the car. She was scared Ned would ruin the weekend for Dad. As if Dad was a baby who had to have everything his own way.

Ned pointed shakily at the beefburgers. "*Murder!*" he bellowed hoarsely, like an angry ghost.

"Stop it, Ned," Rose hissed. "Dad will cook you something else, won't you, Dad?"

But Ned couldn't stop. He clenched his fists. "Do you know what meat is?" he yelled into Dad's startled face. "MURDERED animals. You're cooking MURDER burgers. I hate your GUTS. I'm going home and you can't stop me and I'm never coming back ever AGAIN!"

3: *Welcome to the Real World Hotel*

OF COURSE NED couldn't go home, however much he wanted to. His mum was visiting a friend in another town. He was trapped in this cold empty flat until Sunday night.

Somehow the three of them got through the evening. When Dad and Rose spoke to Ned they used careful voices. As if he were a boy of glass who'd break if they acted normally.

He lay on the prickly matting, pretending to watch TV. Dad and Rose washed up, singing silly songs the way they used to in Osborne Street,

laughing just a bit too much. Probably
they felt they had to be specially
cheerful to make up for Ned.

He was relieved when it was
bedtime. The air-bed was a musty
borrowed one with a wheezy puncture,
but he must have fallen asleep, because
the dream came again. And Ned woke
yelling as he'd been afraid he would.
"Don't go! Don't go!"

Rose trudged off sighing to fetch
their father. Dad emerged in his
pyjamas, looking dazed. He patted
Ned's shoulder awkwardly a couple of
times then said, shivering, "Think you
can sleep now?"

"Yes," lied Ned.

After Dad left, Ned lay listening to the
birds chirping in the half-dawn. He
couldn't believe the things he'd shouted
at Dad. Ned never used to be the

shouting kind. What was happening?

I'm turning into a stranger too, he thought. We're all strangers now.

After breakfast they went to look around the market. Dad found some penknives like small silver fishes and asked Ned if he'd like one.

"All right," said Ned grudgingly, still wanting his revenge for the Murder Burgers.

But taking the knife made him feel even worse. A real Dad would have known Ned had outgrown toy knives years ago.

Then Rose fell loudly in love with a floppy velvet hat.

"I'll treat you," said Dad at once.

Rose put the hat on in the street and twirled around, giggling. "Does it look nice?"

"Beautiful," said Dad. "The same red as Gretta's wallflowers."

Ned trailed along behind them, uneasily fingering his babyish knife, wishing he liked it half as much as his sister liked her silly hat.

They had lunch in a noisy Italian place which served vegetarian food. Ned tried to wind his spaghetti on to his fork but it kept escaping.

Dad said, "What do you want to do next, Ned?"

Rose spluttered Coke down her nose. "How come he gets to choose?"

But Ned chose the ice rink because Mum would never take them.

"Not bad for a squirt," said Rose, impressed.

In the evening Dad tinkered on the piano. Rose and Ned watched TV with the sound down, groaning whenever they moved. Skating was more painful than it looked.

Just one more night, Ned thought, slithering on to his air-bed in the dark. Then he'd be safely back home.

It wasn't that Ned didn't *like* his dad. It was just that he couldn't help wondering now if he and Dad had always been strangers without knowing it. Even in the days when the Garfields had seemed like a normal happy family.

Supposing everything had always been one big lie from beginning to end, and Ned was just too stupid to see?

That night he dreamed. Of shoals of penknives that swam out of reach. Of spaghetti unwinding from a giant fork faster than Ned could eat it. And of a red velvet hat that sailed over the rooftops like a bird till it was lost among the stars.

Something was wrong. Ned sensed it in his sleep. Something was missing.

He wandered anxiously into a warehouse of dreams apparently run by the man who owned the town video shop.

"It must be here," Ned was saying. "My grandad's in it. And some cauliflowers and a bird."

"Another customer's probably borrowed it," said the man unhelpfully.

Ned lost his temper. "That was MY dream," he yelled. "HOW DARE YOU let anyone take it." Then he felt the first rumblings of an enormous earthquake. The dream warehouse started to cave in on him.

Rose was shaking him, yelling, "Breakfast!"

"Go away," said Ned, dazed. "I haven't had my dream."

"I thought you hated that old dream," said Rose impatiently. "There's no pleasing you. Anyway, hurry up. I'm going to clean up the flat for Dad.''

Ned felt terrible. Now he'd lost it, it seemed to him that the dream had been the one thing that was really his.

"There's nothing to do," he moaned. "Why can't I watch telly?"

Dad stood firm. No television in the mornings. "You'll just have to be bored, Ned," he said. "Welcome to the Real World Hotel."

Ned absolutely hated it when Dad said that.

"I'll take you to the park after lunch," Dad promised. He was composing a new song. When Dad had music on his mind, he wouldn't notice if his feet caught fire, Ned thought bitterly. It was no use making a fuss. Ned might as well be invisible.

He couldn't even look out at the

street. The windows were skylights, high in the roof. Today the sky was the colour of weak tea. Storm coloured.

Ned's heart sank. "Don't rain," he whispered.

By eleven the first drops struck the dirty glass like bullets. By twelve a steady waterfall was pouring down both skylights.

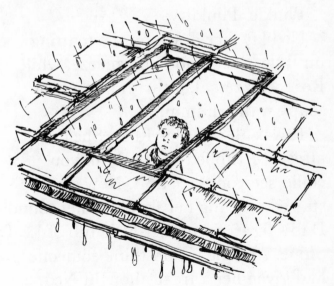

"Rain on Monday instead," Ned prayed. "Rain all week if you want to, but don't, DON'T rain today."

Ned HAD to get Dad out of the flat. He just had to.

Plink plink, went the piano.

Once Ned's father crashed the keys and swore. Another time he muttered, "Oh *yes*! Better."

Plinkle. Plinkitty.

Ned lay face down on the matting until the dust made him sneeze, while Rose whizzed about with buckets of soapy water, humming.

It was all right for Rose. She'd already scrubbed the bath till you could see your face in it. Now she started working her way steadily round Dad's fig tree with her little tub of Leaf Shine. Anyone would think someone had given her a treat, thought Ned, as

she polished away, like little Mrs Tittlemouse.

"Does it look better now, Daddy?" Rose asked, when Dad finally dragged himself away from the piano to make lunch. She showed him the glossy green plant.

Dad was impressed. "I didn't know it was that colour underneath."

He turned to Ned. "Now, old mate,"

he said in a wheedling voice. "Change of plan."

Oh-oh, thought Ned. Using this same persuasive tone Dad had convinced Ned to let doctors stick painful needles in his arm and pour disgusting medicine down his throat.

"As it's turned so wet," Dad said, still using his Ned-charming voice, "there are a couple of films I thought we'd watch, instead. *Singing in the Rain* and – "

"No," said Ned loudly. "No films. You promised."

"Ned," warned Rose.

"We've *got* to go out," wailed Ned. He was behaving like a baby, but he couldn't help it.

"Keep your hair on," said Dad, to Ned's surprise. "We'll go out if you're that desperate. Skin's waterproof after all."

Rose frowned at the streaming skylight. "Rather you than me."

So Ned and his dad went alone.

The streets were almost empty. The cars slooshing past them had their headlights on. It was more like night

than afternoon, as they plodded silently along. Only now that he was out on this dismal day Ned couldn't remember why it had seemed so important to get Dad away from the flat.

He was freezing as well as unhappy. Even with Rose out of the way, Ned couldn't think of anything to say. Dad felt the same, Ned could tell, though he pretended to be cheerful.

'Well, Ned, Spring's been postponed,'' he announced, inspecting his left shoe which had sprung a leak. ''This rain's turning to sleet. But what do we care?'' He twizzled round a lamp post. ''Doodee doo doo – Just singing in the rain . . . ''

Ned didn't join in. His teeth were rattling in his jaw like a skeleton's.

''Want to head back home?'' asked

Dad, looking hopeful.

"Not yet," said Ned obstinately. Why was he so sure they mustn't go back? It wasn't just to punish Dad. For moving away. For cooking Murder Burgers. For ignoring Ned all morning until it was too wet to go to the park.

There was another more important reason. A crazy notion, that had put itself into his head as clearly as if someone had whispered a promise.

If Ned could only keep Dad out of the house long enough, something might happen.

Something that would make everything all right again.

"Okay, let's walk into town," sighed his dad, leaping back as a car whooshed past spraying mud.

They trudged on, heads down against the sleet.

41

Dad stuffed his hands bravely in his pockets and turned up his collar as far as it would go, but his face looked blue.

Ned's ears burned. His feet were lumps of ice.

But it still wasn't time to go home.

There were more people in town. They looked miserable too. It was that sort of Sunday.

Dad peered through the windows of the launderette. "Looks warm in there," he said enviously. "Wish I'd brought my shirts. Look at those wimps, Ned. Brollies *and* coats. Call themselves men. Pah!"

Ned turned his giggle into a cough, then laughed outright. It was almost impossible not to laugh at Dad, even when you were mad at him.

Dad grinned back lopsidedly out

of his blue face.

"How come Purdy's have *exactly* the same cakes in their window," Ned puzzled as they passed the bakers, "year after year. It's sinister if you ask me."

"I'm freezing, Ned," said Dad, jogging on the spot.

"Must be cunningly painted plaster fakes," Ned decided.

"*Ned*," implored Dad, gibbering now.

But Ned was inspecting Purdy's lurid apple turnovers and didn't hear.

A howling wind swept down the street. The sleet turned to bouncing pellets of hail. Cursing, Dad ducked into the doorway of the Singer shop.

Then he called urgently, "Ned, look at this." And in a softer voice, "Well *you're* too small to be out without your mum."

His dad had found some little lost kid, Ned decided.

Great, that was all they needed.

But in the doorway, inches from the tramping feet of passers-by, there was only an ugly baby bird.

Ned had never seen anything die

before, but he knew at once that this little bird was dying. Its eyes kept closing. Almost too weak to stand, it quivered like a shabby leaf at each gust of hail.

"Fallen out of its nest," said Dad, craning his neck. "There's the mother, look."

Ned peered upwards. A bird flew in frantic circles overhead.

45

"She daren't come closer," said Dad. "But the nest is too far up to climb." He tested the drainpipe, shaking his head. "And this little bloke isn't nearly old enough to feed himself."

"We can't do anything, can we," said Ned angrily. Ned had been so sure something wonderful would happen while he and his dad were out on their own. And *now* look.

He stared at the ugly little bird tottering blindly in the doorway. His eyes filled. "It's not fair," he muttered fiercely.

Dad shook his head again and Ned knew what he was going to say: "Welcome to the Real World Hotel."

Only Ned's father didn't say a word. He crouched down, scooping the fledgling gently into his hand.

Then he popped it in his pocket.

Ned's mouth opened and shut. Dad had just kidnapped a baby bird!

The mother bird wheeled around their heads screaming. Passers-by stared. Only Dad looked calm, as if he

pocketed baby birds every day of the
week.

"Come on," he said to Ned. "Maybe
we can't save him. But we can spare
him some suffering. Let's take him
home to Rose."

4: *"Birds Don't Belong in Boxes"*

"YOU'VE BEEN AGES," complained
Rose. "The lady downstairs brought us
some things for tea," she added,
without taking her eyes off the TV
screen. "They look funny but they
taste nice. Gretta's sweet."

Ned didn't want to hear about Gretta.
"We found a baby bird," he stammered.
"It's in Dad's pocket. It's dying."

Rose jumped up. "Show me."

Dad balanced the fledgling on his
palm. It shuddered gently to and fro
on tiny reptile's claws, its eyes sealed
shut.

49

Rose stroked its greasy head. "Poor little bird. You've lost your mum and dad. And pooh, you really pong. But that's not your fault," she added kindly.

"It doesn't know where it is," whispered Ned. "It doesn't know anything now. That's why it's not scared."

"We couldn't let it die in the street," explained Dad.

"We need a box for him," said Ned.

Rose frowned. "To die in, you mean?"

"I've got a shoe box somewhere," said Dad.

Ned shredded newspaper to make a soft bed.

Still frowning, Rose lowered the fledgling. It crumpled on its side at once and lay still. Ned looked away.

Rose shook her head. "This isn't
right. Birds don't belong in boxes."

"It's dying, Rose," Ned whispered.
"It won't care."

"I'd care," said Rose in her normal
bossy voice, "if I was a bird."

"Leave it in peace, kids," said Dad.
"Let's see what Gretta's brought for
tea."

"I couldn't," said Ned.

"Nor me," said Rose. Both children stared at their father in horror.

Dad sighed. "Me neither," he admitted. "But I need a cuppa to thaw my bones." He vanished into his kitchen.

"We could play hangman," suggested Rose. "To take our minds off things."

Ned shrugged, surprised. "I don't mind." Rose hadn't played with him for months.

They played paper-and-pencil games with the telly on low out of respect. There was a gangster film on.

"You got a noive, Charlie, to do that," said a gangster, out of the side of his rubbery mouth. "You got a *real* noive."

Dad tinkered half-heartedly with his song. Plink. Plinketty.

Rose frowned at the silent mound of feathers beside them, but Ned was ashamed to watch the little bird die. He had a spiky lump in his throat, making it hurt to swallow.

Suddenly Rose threw her pencil across the floor.

"What's wrong?" asked Ned, alarmed.

"Everything!" shouted Rose angrily. She had tears in her eyes.

Reaching her hand into the box she plucked out the dying bird.

"Leave it, Rose," protested Ned.

"Yes," said Dad, crashing chords. "For Heaven's sake."

"Honestly," muttered Rose, furious. "Men are such quitters." Still muttering, she marched across the matting with the bird.

Ned wanted to murder her. "What are you DOING!" he shrieked. The fledgling was nothing to do with Rose. It was his and Dad's. Rose just couldn't bear Ned to have something of his own. Not even an ugly little half-dead bird.

"Doing?" Rose shrieked back, enormous tears rolling down her face.

She shoved the lifeless lump of feathers into the fig tree. "THIS," she yelled at him, "THIS is what I'm doing."

They glared at each other, trembling.

"This is the worst thing you've ever done, Rose," said Ned, sick with horror, waiting for the dying bird to hit the ground like a little heap of dirty rags.

Instead he heard a faint fluttering among the leaves.

Then a tiny but distinct chirp.

Ned stared. "But it was . . . "

"Rose Garfield," said Dad, grumpily leaving his piano. "Didn't you hear what your brother s – ?"

But Rose was beaming with happiness. "Dad," she whispered, "isn't it *lucky* you had the tree. Now he'll be all right. I know he will."

The bird stood bolt upright, clasping his twig as though glued there.

"He's opening his eyes!" Ned breathed.

Bright brown beads stared back with interest.

"Hello, bird," said Ned, his heart thudding. He stretched out his hand.

"Heavens!" giggled Rose.

The fledgling's beak had flown open.

Ned stared down a long throat as pink and vivid as a tropical flower.

"Chirp," said the baby bird hopefully. "Chirp chirp."

"He wants you to feed him," Rose told Ned.

Ned felt worried. "I don't know what he eats."

"Try Weetabix."

Ned hurtled back with milky cereal in a saucer. He poked a fingerful towards the ridged pink tunnel of the baby bird's throat. It grabbed at the stodgy mess. "Watch it," Ned warned. "My finger isn't included in your dinner, you know."

"I've seen prettier gargoyles than that little tweetie bird," said Dad rudely.

Ned wasn't fooled. He knew Dad was thrilled the bird had decided not to die.

"So what are we calling him?" Dad joked. "Quasimodo? Frankenstein?"

"His name's Ugly Mug," said Ned quickly, before Rose could come up with something girly.

"Poor thing," said Rose, appalled. "*Why?*"

Ned gave a sideways look at Dad. "Because he's a gangster bird."

Dad laughed. "Ugly Mug it is, then," he said, ruffling Ned's hair. Then, in his gangster's voice, "Ugly Mug, the Back-street Boid."

"Oh, you got a noive, Charlie," said Ned, grinning at him. "You got a *real* noive to say that."

5: *Flying Lessons*

"THE SINGER SHOP," said Mum, tickled, as she drove home. "That's a good place to find a bird."

"It's only a sparrow, Mum," said Rose. "Sparrows just chirp, you know. They don't sing. They can't."

"How long will your orphan be living in Dad's tree?"

"Till he can look after himself," said Ned firmly. "Dad promised."

"Aren't you glad you went now, Ned?" asked Mum. She looked miles better for her weekend away, Ned noticed.

"Except for the Murder Burgers he is," said Rose slyly. Ned waited for her to snitch to Mum about how awful he'd been. But she didn't. She just grinned behind Mum's back and after a second or two, uncertainly, Ned grinned back.

Ned phoned Dad the minute he got back from school next day.

Dad sounded worn out. "I don't know how your mum coped with you two. One loud greedy bird is more than enough for me."

Dad's phone was a shared one on the stairs. Ned could hear footsteps and chatter from a radio. He could picture where Dad was now. It helped somehow.

"Gretta says we should give him raw mince," Dad added.

"Yuck," said Ned.

"You can't expect a growing gangster to live on Weetabix," said Dad.

"I suppose not," Ned agreed.

"Do you know," said Dad, "at night he creeps into the middle of the tree and hides. I had to look hard to find him and I knew he was there. He turns himself into a tiny shadow."

Ned smiled into the receiver. "That's in case your room changes into gangster territory while he's asleep," he said.

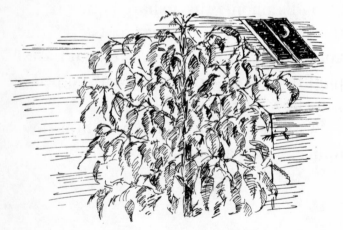

"It nearly did. I caught Gretta's cat sneaking across the landing."

Ned's smile vanished. "Did you shut your door when you answered the phone?"

"What do *you* think? I'm not running a freebie snack bar for cats, you know."

Ned giggled. "Can we come and see Ugly soon?"

"Come on Wednesday, if your mum doesn't mind. And before you say it, I promise Murder Burgers will never darken my kitchen again . . . "

"Ugly's bigger," said Rose on Wednesday evening. "And not so bald." She sniffed the air. "Not quite so smelly, either."

"He's still got a funny gangster's mouth," said Ned, puzzled. "Sort of painted on, like a clown's."

"Gretta says fledglings have those markings to make it easier for their mums to feed them," explained Dad.

And she's a nosy cow, thought Ned jealously. But then Ugly Mug's beak split open hopefully again like a trick flower, exposing that long greedy pink tunnel, and he laughed.

"He's making a horrible mess." Ned pointed at the chalky splashes on the leaves of the fig tree.

"I try to think of it as free fertilizer," said Dad airily.

"What about when he's flying round the room?"

Dad grinned his lopsided grin. "There's not much furniture to damage."

"Hey," said Rose. "Look what he can do. Do it again, Ugly." She held out her hand. "Da-da!" she sang.

With a chirp the baby sparrow stepped on to her finger and clung there calmly, just like a tame canary.

"Let me," said Ned jealously.

"Keep your hair on," said Rose. "Put your finger close, like this, and he'll just hop on. Look! He can't help himself!"

"Oh, his feet feel *weird*," said Ned. "Just like they did in my dr – "

His eyes widened. His mouth fell open.

"What's the matter?" asked Dad.

"You look as if you've seen a ghost."

"I did, I saw one in my dream," said Ned at last, banging himself on the chest. "The one I had every night since you and Mum – told us, you know. Until we found Ugly. Only in my dream Grandad Garfield gave me the bird."

Then Ned knew why he'd had to drag Dad out in the storm that day and who had put that promise in his head.

Magic. That's what Grandad had wanted Ned to remember. That however lonely you are, and however terrible things seem, magic can still come to you, if you look for it. Maybe Ned's magic wasn't like the dramatic starburst and mysterious music kind you got in books, but Ugly Mug was exactly what he'd needed. Somehow, because he still loved Ned, Grandad had made that magic happen.

A few days later Rose answered the phone.

"Ugly's learning to fly," she told Ned. "Dad says he's not very good. Let's give him some flying practice before tea. Oh, if you don't mind, Mum." She shot a worried glance at her mother. Rose was having loads more fun these days so sometimes she forgot to be helpful, but Mum didn't seem to mind.

"I want to hear how Ugly's getting on as much as you do," Mum said.

It was Ned who discovered the best way to teach Ugly to fly. He tossed him into the air just inches from Rose so he didn't have far to fall. The bird only managed short distances at first but soon they were whizzing him from one to the other like a fantastic game of paper aeroplanes. By teatime both Rose and Ned were pink and breathless.

"We'd better come tomorrow," said Rose bossily. "So Ugly doesn't forget what he's learned. We don't want him to be a backward bird just because he's an orphan. Promise you'll remember his lunchtime lessons, Dad?"

"Aye, aye," said Dad, saluting.

By the following week Ugly was increasingly expert.

Dad came out of the kitchen to watch. "I'm not sure you should be *whizzing* him," he said doubtfully.

"He *loves* it," said Ned. "He flies further every time, don't you, Ugly? Put out your arm, Rose, or he'll miss."

Gently he shook the little bird

into the air again.

Ugly Mug whirred confidently across the room, staying airborne until he reached Rose. But instead of perching on her arm, at the last minute he soared upwards, landing on her head and flapping his wings with a deafening cheep of triumph.

Dad laughed. "He's pleased with himself."

"Help," said Rose. "Get him off before he does something disgusting.

His feet feel horrible walking about on my head!"

They ate supper at Dad's new table.

"What do you think of my soup?" asked Dad.

"Nice," said Rose politely.

"Not bad," said Ned, piling on salt. "Well, better than the last lot," he added kindly.

Dad smiled. "Maybe my song will make our fortunes and you'll never have to eat my leek and potato soup again."

"I expect Ugly Mug inspired you," said Rose loftily. "With the song, I mean not the soup, oh – I didn't mean – !" She clapped her hand to her mouth. But Dad only laughed again and she grinned with relief.

"Do you know what that little bird did? He settled beside me with his feet tucked underneath him just like a tiny hen. Then he looked me in the eye, man to man, well *boid* to man, with such a wise expression. As if he knew perfectly well Ned and I rescued him."

"He does know," said Ned confidently.

"Oh, I wish *I'd* seen him," said Rose. "He's turned himself into a little shadow in his tree now till morning."

"There's always the weekend," said Dad. "It's my turn to have you, isn't it? Why the long face, Ned? Don't you want to come? No Murder Burgers, cross my heart! I'm a changed man. I've even bought a vegetarian cookery book."

"It's not that," said Ned unhappily. "It's Ugly. When he can fly properly we'll have to let him go, won't we? And we'll never see him again."

And Dad's flat will turn back into an aircraft hangar, he thought, and Rose will shut me out of everything again the way she did before.

Grandad's magic will be over.

But this time it would be over for good. And Ned would be more alone than ever.

6: Singing in the Dark

NED KNEW AS soon as Dad got out of the car.

"He's different," said Dad, putting their bags in the boot. "Sort of restless."

That evening, Ugly refused to play paper aeroplanes. He couldn't settle, flitting from one part of the room to another, cheeping anxiously. Several times he flew up to the skylights, hovering against the glass as if he was trying to find his way out into the twilight.

"He wants to be free," said Ned,

73

his chest tight with sadness.

"We'll take him into the garden tomorrow," said Dad. "I know it's hard, Ned, but we've got no choice."

Ned knew Dad was right.

It was the first time Ned had been in the garden. He'd pictured a yard with overflowing bins and was surprised by the daffodils and blue pools of forget-me-nots under the trees.

Rose carried the sparrow out of the house. She held out her open palm with the bright-eyed bird balanced on it.

"Goodbye, Ugly," said Ned bravely, expecting Ugly to whiz into the air right away.

But except for his feathers ruffling in the wind, Ugly stayed motionless, astonished at this amazing world without walls. He cocked his head, apparently listening to the wind and the birdsong in the gardens around them.

Then slowly the bird began to rotate on Rose's outstretched hand, as if he wanted to see and hear this new world from every possible angle.

"Like a little radar scanner," said Dad softly.

"He keeps stopping and looking and listening," breathed Rose.

Suddenly Ugly opened his beak and chirped loudly. Then he returned to his slow, circling dance, only now,

each time he stopped, he chirped
loudly again before moving on.

"He's calling his mum and brothers
and sisters," said Rose.

"It's all right, Ugly," said Ned.
"You can go. You're free. Let him go,
Rose," he begged, wanting to get it
over with.

Rose flipped her hand.

But the sparrow only flew round her

head in a tight circle, landing back on her shoulder.

"You're free," repeated Ned anxiously. "You're a grown-up bird now. You can go."

Again Rose tossed Ugly into the air. This time he came to Ned with a soft whirring of his wings, settling on his head.

"He won't go," said Ned in tears. "What's wrong?"

"Perhaps he's not ready," said Dad. "Try again tomorrow."

Maybe they'd made Ugly too tame, Ned worried. Maybe he wouldn't be able to survive outside now like other birds.

As they took the sparrow back into the house Ned glimpsed a white-haired woman bustling about in the basement. Gretta's mother had come

77

to stay, he thought.

In the afternoon Dad took them to
the cinema. They bought fish and
chips on the way home. While Dad
unwrapped them, Ned whistled to
Ugly to come and play. He was acting
more restless than ever, flying again
and again to the skylights, cheeping
and beating his wings against the glass
as if he was trying to reach the brilliant
colours of the sunset beyond.

But when it grew dark, Ugly
vanished secretively into his fig tree as
usual.

For all his worries, Ned felt peaceful.
It was nice sitting with Dad, talking
about the film they'd seen together,
sharing chips that were still just a little
bit too hot, watching the colours fade
in the sky.

Then it happened. One by one the

sweet, husky notes stole around them
like a halting tune played on a tiny
reed flute.

Rose stopped, a chip half-way to her
mouth, her eyes enormous. "It's Ugly.
He's *singing*."

Ned forgot to breathe. "But you said
sparrows don't. They can't."

"Ssh," said Dad. "This might never

happen again for a thousand years. Just listen." He reached out, taking their hands in his.

They sat in the gathering shadows, their chips growing cold, as Ugly Mug's voice, stronger and more confident with every moment, filled the room.

A new moon like a baby's finger nail rose in the sky.

In the flat next door someone switched on a TV and filled a kettle.

But still the little bird went on singing.

Ned thought his heart would burst. He wanted the three of them to sit in the dark listening to Ugly singing for ever.

When he stopped at last they stirred, rubbing their eyes as if coming out of a dream. Like sleep-walkers they took their greasy plates into the kitchen. No one wanted lights, so Dad lit candles. Then Dad played the piano and Rose and Ned hummed along.

And somehow, without knowing *how* he knew, Ned knew things were going to be all right from now on.

Next morning before anyone else was up, he and Rose crept down to the damp grey garden and placed Ugly on the twig of a rambler rose.

"You're on your own now," said Ned sternly. "No more Weetabix or flying lessons. Think you can cope all by yourself?"

The sparrow clung to his twig,
gazing back, bright-eyed.

Rose gripped Ned's sleeve, her face
wet.

They went into the house without
looking back.

When they came down again after
half an hour, Ugly had gone.

A few days later Ned dropped in to see
Dad on his way back from the dentist.
But Dad's door was locked and no one
answered Ned's calls.

He was going to give up and go
home when a door opened downstairs.
A soft foreign-sounding voice called
Ned's name.

Ned stumped down again scowling.
So he was finally going to meet *her*, was
he? But it wasn't the girlfriend after
all. It was her plump, white-haired

mother smiling in the doorway of the garden flat.

"Your dad had to pop out, Ned," said the lady. "He asked me to hang on to you until he got back. If you like I'll find you something to eat, but first I have to hang some washing out."

Ned followed her. "Is it Gretta who looks after this garden?" he asked reluctantly. He had to admit she did it well. Every corner was loved and cared for.

"But my dear, I *am* Gretta," the lady said, surprised.

"Oh, I see," said Ned, blushing. He felt a complete idiot. "I didn't think you were so – I mean I thought you were – "

Gretta laughed aloud. "And now *I* see," she said, pegging some very large flowery knickers on the line. "I promise you, your father and I are just good friends who sometimes help each other in hard times. Of course you realise, Ned, that one day he may find some new lady, but we were not meant to live in this world alone."

"I know," said Ned, blushing. "I don't want him to be lonely, either." He wanted to say that it wasn't the idea of girlfriends he'd minded, so much as the way his old life had turned upside-down. And the way his dad had got himself a strange new life that didn't seem to have much room in it for Ned. Gretta seemed to understand.

"The best changes always make the world a *bigger* place, with *more* happiness for everyone, not less," she said comfortably. "I am your father's friend, but I'd like to be your friend

too, Ned. So, are you ready for
something to eat? There's coffee cake
in my larder."

That's when it happened.

Of course Ned had no way of
knowing if it was *his* sparrow. But why
would any other bird swoop out of the
apple tree and fly round their heads
chirping so excitedly?

Why would a strange sparrow fly so
close to Ned it practically parted his
hair, then veer off into the sky, still
chirping?

Why?

Ned gazed after the disappearing
bird until his eyes hurt. "It *was* Ugly,"
he said softly. "He came to tell me he's
all right."

Gretta laid her hand on his shoulder. "Ready for that cake?"

Ned nodded, his eyes still fixed on that little dot in the sky.

"See you, Ugly," he whispered. "See you around, Schweetheart."

And then he went indoors with Gretta to wait for Dad.